The Christmas Coat

Memories of My Sioux Childhood

by Virginia Driving Hawk Sneve

illustrated by Ellen Beier

Holiday House / New York

HOLIDAY HOUSE is registered in the U.S. Patent Trademark Office.
Printed and bound in April 2011 at Kwong Fat Offset Printing Co., Ltd., Dongguan City, China.
The text typeface is Breughel.
The illustrations were done in watercolor and gouache on Fabriano watercolor paper.
www.holidayhouse.com
First Edition
1 3 5 7 9 10 8 6 4 2

Library of Congress Cataloging-in-Publication Data
The Christmas coat : memories of my Sioux childhood / by Virginia Driving Hawk Sneve ;
illustrated by Ellen Beier. — 1st ed.
p. cm.
ISBN 978-0-8234-2134-3 (hardcover)
1. Sneve, Virginia Driving Hawk.
2. Dakota Indians—Biography.
I. Beier, Ellen. II. Title.
PS3569.N474Z46 2011
813'.54—dc22
[B]
2010029562

To Rose, my mother,
who taught me to think of others
who needed more than I
V. D. H. S.

For Charles and Samuel
E. B.

THE FRIGID GALE BLEW SIDEWAYS across the South Dakota prairie, and cold rain lashed the children's bare faces. They leaned into it to stay upright on the reservation road to school. Squishy slime sucked at their rubber overshoes. Eddie Driving Hawk's left overshoe stuck in the gumbo.

"Aaah, sister! Help!" he cried as he grabbed Virginia's arm, trying to keep his sock out of the mud.

"I've got you." Virginia steadied the little boy while Marty Brokenleg freed the overshoe.

"If I had cowboy boots, they wouldn't have come out of the overshoes," Eddie grumbled.

The children trudged on. Virginia shivered. She pulled her mittens up and tugged the coat's sleeves down in a vain attempt to cover her bare wrists. I need a new coat, she thought, and slipped into a daydream. Maybe a red one that wasn't tight across her chest and that was long enough to reach the tops of her overshoes. It would have a warm hood. . . .

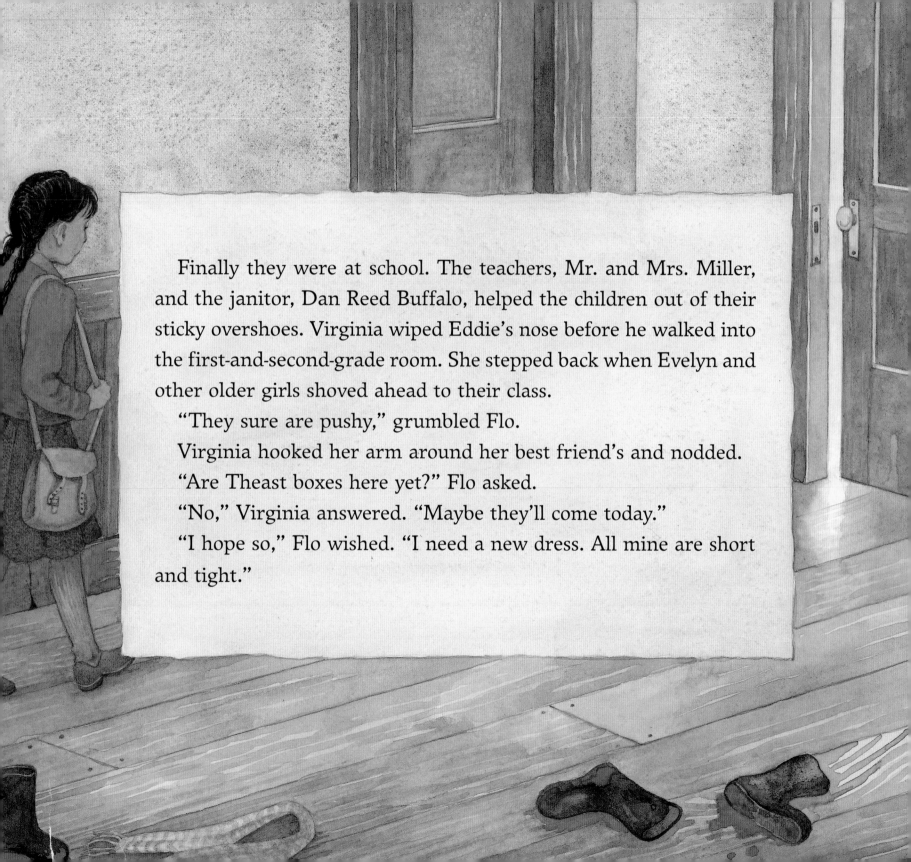

Finally they were at school. The teachers, Mr. and Mrs. Miller, and the janitor, Dan Reed Buffalo, helped the children out of their sticky overshoes. Virginia wiped Eddie's nose before he walked into the first-and-second-grade room. She stepped back when Evelyn and other older girls shoved ahead to their class.

"They sure are pushy," grumbled Flo.

Virginia hooked her arm around her best friend's and nodded.

"Are Theast boxes here yet?" Flo asked.

"No," Virginia answered. "Maybe they'll come today."

"I hope so," Flo wished. "I need a new dress. All mine are short and tight."

All through the day Virginia kept thinking about Theast boxes. *Theast* meant "The East," and referred to large cartons of used clothing, shoes, and other items sent by church congregations in New England. The boxes arrived in the fall with winter clothes and in the spring with summer things.

Virginia and Eddie never got first pick from the boxes, because their father was the Episcopal priest of the village, and as Mama always said, "The others need it more than we do."

Virginia's coat was so small because last year it had been the only one left that fit her, and it had been short then.

By the time the school day ended, the rain and wind had stopped, and the gumbo was easier to walk through. Theast boxes had arrived, and Mrs. Little Money and Mrs. High Bear helped Mama sort the items. Virginia looked for the pile of clothing in her size but saw no coats. But later that evening when it was just the Driving Hawks in the rummage room, she spotted a coat in her size. It was a shimmering gray fur with a satiny silver lining.

"Ooh!" Her hand reached to stroke the fur, but she determinedly turned away. She knew someone else would get it. It was too beautiful.

"Look, a tuxedo." Dad held up a black suit. He put it on and laughed at how it bagged about his shoulders. "And here are the shoes." He wiggled his toes into shiny black pumps.

"Shall we dance, madam?" he invited Mama, who tossed a ragged lacy shawl over her shoulders. They twirled through the room to polka music from radio station WNAX. Virginia pulled on a white gown and whirled after her parents.

"What's this?" Eddie held up a stiff white thing.

"A corset," Mama said.

"For fat ladies," Dad said, fastening it about his middle and waltzing Virginia across the floor.

"Uh, oh," Dad whispered as the door opened.

"Well, humph! I never—" Mrs. Red Buffalo glared at the dancers and stomped from the room.

"Now we're in trouble," Dad said. "The whole village will know that the priest wears a corset when he dances."

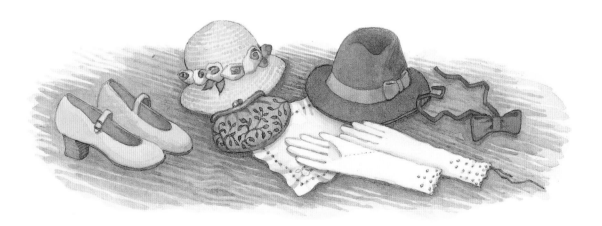

Saturday came, and the rummage room was filled. First the mothers with babies and young children, then the children, and then the adults. Virginia sat by the door and helped watch babies while their mamas sorted through the clothes. She kept an eye on the gray fur coat. Freda looked at it, but it was too long. Others stroked it, but their mamas said no. So Virginia began to hope no one would take it.

Evelyn tramped in with her sisters. "Oh, I hope there's good stuff left!" she cried. "We had to push the car out of the gumbo." She headed for the coats.

"I need a new coat; mine's way too—ooh!" She'd spotted the gray fur.

Virginia gulped back the lump in her throat. On her lap, the baby cried as she squeezed him tight.

She rocked to comfort the baby and watched Evelyn slip into the coat. "It's perfect. Isn't it beautiful? And it fits!"

Virginia hid her tears in the baby's soft hair.

Later that afternoon, the Driving Hawks chose their winter clothes. Mama found a drab brown coat that was a bit too big for Virginia. The sleeves and hem would need to be shortened. Until then she'd have to wear the old green one.

It was so hard to follow Evelyn and her friends on the walk to school. "I just love the way my fur coat feels. It's so soft, and the label inside says it's *lapin*."

Virginia wrapped her arms around her chest, trying to hold in her jealousy. In the classroom she asked Mr. Miller what *lapin* meant.

"Hmm," he said. "It's been a while since I used my French, but I believe it means rabbit."

"Thank you," Virginia said.

Another wet, sleety, cold day came; and again the children trudged through the squishy gumbo. Virginia followed the older girls and heard Evelyn cry "Oh, no!" as she tried to keep the fur coat out of the slime.

In the cloakroom Evelyn slipped out of the fur and shook muddy drops onto the floor. "Oh, this wonderful coat kept me warm and dry."

The familiar wet, woolly aroma filled the air, but now there was a reek of . . . of?

The children sniffed and looked around.

"Pee-youie!" Marty exclaimed. "Evelyn, your coat stinks. I think a dog died in it!"

Everyone laughed.

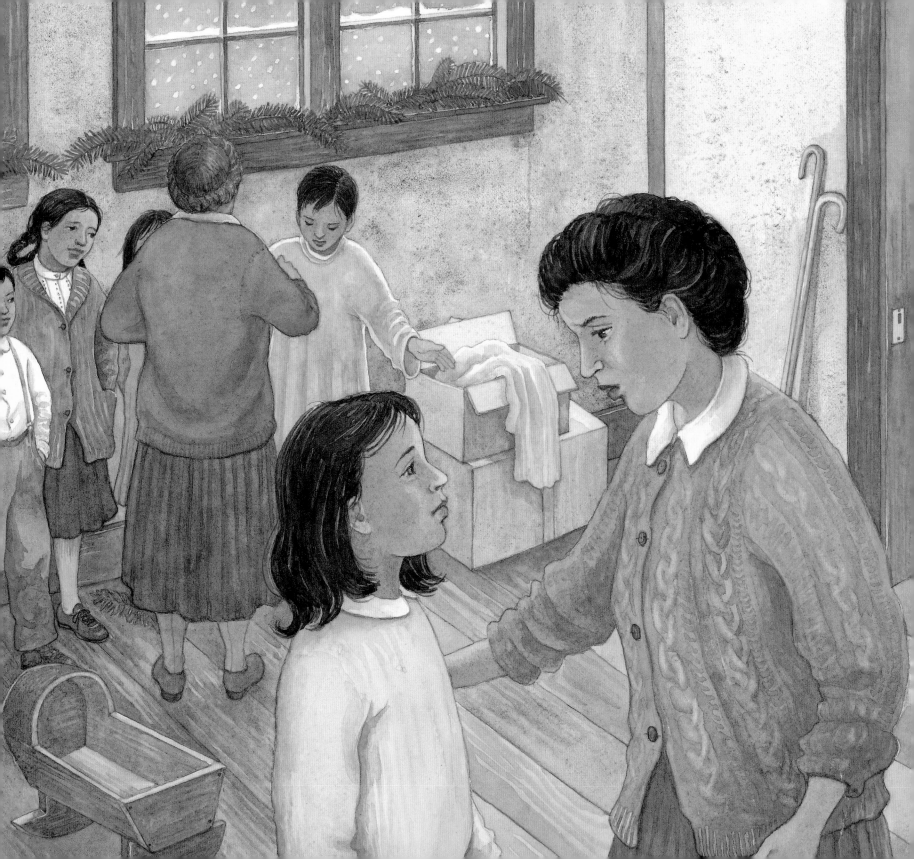

Christmas was near, and after school the children went to the guildhall for pageant and carol practice. Mama called Virginia over before she joined the others.

"Evelyn needs another coat. Her mother said the fur one isn't practical to wear to school," Mama explained.

"And it smells like a dog." Virginia smirked.

"That's not a nice thing to say," Mama warned.

Virginia stayed silent while Mama went on. "The only other coat that fit her was the brown one you have. It's a good thing I didn't get it hemmed and you haven't worn it to school yet."

Virginia frowned. She didn't like the coat, but she hated the thought of Evelyn getting it.

"I'm sorry." Mama patted Virginia's shoulder. "But . . ."

Through gritted teeth, Virginia said with Mama, "She needs it more than we do."

Virginia moved aimlessly through the Christmas preparations. She didn't care. It was no fun. On Christmas Eve the congregation gathered in the guildhall around a huge Christmas tree. Colorful paper chains and shiny tinsel glittered among the large white handkerchiefs and smaller, multicolored ones tucked in branches. Every man and woman would get one.

Eddie was a shepherd in the Nativity pageant and proudly knelt before the cradle, where a doll lay wrapped in a baby star quilt.

Virginia was happy that Flo was Mary in a blue gown from one of the Theast boxes. There was a long pause before the Wise Men entered. The whole guildhall seemed to give a big *ahhh* as Marty led two other boys into the hall. They wore headdresses that only the wise leaders and elders of the tribe could wear.

Dad rose to lead the applause as the pageant ended.

"Listen!" he said, holding his hand to his ear. "What's that?"

The room grew quiet to hear horses and shouts of "Whoa!"

Feet stomped and thumped outside. The door burst open, and some of the little kids screamed in fright and their mamas had to calm them. "It's all right. He's Santa Claus!"

Each child got a dolly, ball, or toy car, as well as a paper bag full of candy, peanuts, and an apple from Santa's bag.

After a supper of corn soup, fry bread, and *wojape*, or chokecherry pudding, the congregation walked to the white church on the hill for the Christmas Eve service.

Dad had already left, but Mama and the children went to their house to get blankets to take to church. It would be cold at the midnight service, even with the coal stove.

Mama came with two white boxes and said, "Sometimes the congregations in the East send boxes especially for the priest and his family. They ask what the family needs the most and then they try to send those items.

"Here, Eddie." She gave him a box.

"What is it?" he asked, pulling at the lid. "Oh!" he exclaimed, and pulled out a pair of cowboy boots. Soon both feet were shod in the new boots.

All the while Eddie was trying on his boots, Virginia carefully took the long box Mama gave her and put it on the table. She took a deep breath and opened the box.

A coat! Not a fur one, but a smooth and soft red one. It even had a hood. She looked up at Mama and felt tears in her eyes. She couldn't say anything.

"Try it on," Mama urged.

It was wonderful! A little long in the sleeves and hem, but that was okay.

Virginia buttoned the coat. Tears brimmed, but she smiled. "Thank you, Mama."

"Merry Christmas." Mama smiled back.

"Merry Christmas," Virginia whispered, and tied the hood around her head. The trim of brown fur was soft against her face.

◈